The Week Mom Unplugged the TVs

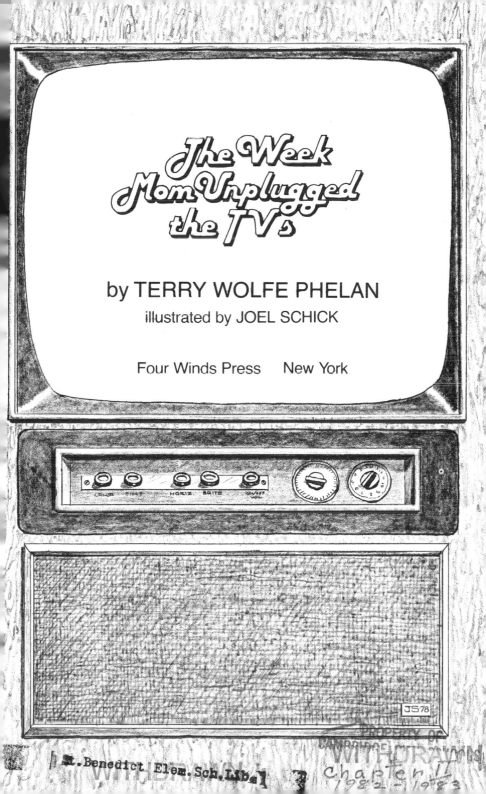

The Week Mom Unplugged the TVs

by TERRY WOLFE PHELAN

illustrated by JOEL SCHICK

Four Winds Press　　New York

Library of Congress Cataloging in Publication Data

Phelan, Terry Wolfe.
    The week mom unplugged the TVs.

    Summary: A parental ban on all television viewing for one
week stimulates the curiosity of three youngsters.
    [1. Play—Fiction.   2. Television—Fiction.   3. Family life—
Fiction]   I. Schick, Joel.   II. Title.
PZ7.P4489We   [Fic]   78-12180
ISBN 0-590-07561-6

Published by Four Winds Press
A division of Scholastic Magazines, Inc., New York, N.Y.
Text copyright © 1979 by Terry Phelan
Illustrations copyright © 1979 by Pongid Productions
All rights reserved
Printed in the United States of America
Library of Congress Catalog Card Number: 78-12180
1   2   3   4   5   83   82   81   80   79

TO

Arnie, Jackie & Becca

WHOSE
ENCOURAGEMENT, ENTHUSIASM
AND TV WATCHING
MADE THIS BOOK POSSIBLE

Contents

Sunday

e had three televisions in our house. We weren't really rich, just lucky. The first TV we bought—like everyone else. My oldest sister Beth won the second TV in a raffle. And the third TV we got when the hospital was giving away their old ones to anyone willing to lug a two-ton set home. So we had to watch shows with snowflakes and zig-zags running through the picture.

No one had to fight about a program or take turns. We just turned on another TV. I ignored my sisters and they ignored me.

Beth liked the soap operas. She was into all that life-and-death stuff. Even if she missed one soap episode, some character would conveniently be hospitalized the next day, so she could still have a good cry.

My middle sister, Stacey, watched the game shows. She's the intellectual type. She even called in when they asked the home viewers questions. I bet she'll grow up to be a professional contestant. She sure is smart enough.

I watched cartoons—even the black and white ones from the olden days. I liked the action. No matter how lousy I did on a math test, when I got home from school and turned on a good cartoon chase, I felt better. I just forgot what 5×8 equals and rooted for Mighty Mouse or Underdog or any superhero that happened to be battling at the moment.

Once in a while we watched reruns — in separate rooms, of course.

But one day, Mom went crazy! "You're all zombies — not people," she said. "You spend all your waking hours glued to the TV screen. I can't stand it anymore. I'm going to pull out all the plugs."

We just stared. We couldn't believe what we were hearing. Then Beth began to sob, "I'm in the middle of a great serial. I can't stop now. I'll never know who Bob loves — Mary, Joan or Francine." Mom just shrugged. I didn't think that was a great argument either. Who cares who Bob loves?

Stacey's argument was better. "I learn so much from the game shows," she said. "I've even learned the capital of Estonia. It's Tallinn." I was impressed. I'd never even heard of Estonia. But Mom wasn't impressed. "Out! Out come the TV plugs!" she hollered.

I already knew Mom hated what I watched. "Cartoons are reruns," she'd say, "and they're all the same. How can you sit there and actually enjoy them?" But she never before unplugged my TV. She didn't even change the channel. I knew I had to try something different to change her mind.

"Ma," I said. "I'm only ten. I like cartoon stories. And to me the reruns are new. I never saw Lucy the first time it was on. And some of the shows I watch even won Emmys." I figured she'd be impressed with the awards. No dice. Mom was determined to unplug.

She headed for the upstairs TV first. Somehow we knew we had only one chance left to save our TVs. We all ran to Dad for support. "Don't give us the argument you grew up without a TV and survived," Stacey said. "This is the twentieth century and television is the American way of life." Wow! I thought, what a good line Stacey had there. My father would never go along with Mom's idea. He would want us to be a

typical American family for sure.

I should have known better. Dad was married to Mom, not to us. He thought Mom was right. "Let's try it for the school week and see what happens," he said.

"Maybe," Mom shouted from upstairs, "maybe we'll become a real family again!"

I couldn't imagine a day without watching TV. And I had to go until Friday at sundown without my shows. It was the worst punishment a parent could give a kid. And I didn't even do anything wrong. I thought no afternoon snack was a bad punishment, but no TV makes an afternoon without a snack look like Easy Street. Mom was a rat and Dad was a rat's husband.

Day 1

om got the upstairs TV that Sunday, but the official pulling out of the plugs began on Monday. I invited every friend I had to my house on Monday. I needed them to forget what I was missing on TV.

At three o'clock, Jimmy, Gary,

Mike, Dave, Fred, George and Bobby arrived. Eight kids made my room feel like the size of a dog house. So we moved to the kitchen. My friends and I drank all the milk, ate our whole stock of Yankee Doodles and used up all the napkins. But Mom only said, smiling, "Glad to have you all here."

When my friends left at five o'clock, all the quiet got to me, so I screamed. It didn't do any good. Mom ignored me. Stacey and Beth ignored my screaming, too. You'd think I went around screaming all my life, the way nobody paid any attention to me.

Then I just sat there in silence. I heard some crickets clicking outside. I'd never heard crickets in the afternoon before. I went to the window and tried to see those clickers in the front lawn. I looked hard. But no matter how hard I stared, I couldn't see them. So I walked around the house sixteen times, and wondered if the cats were still bopping the mice on the 5:30 TV show. I felt like bopping my mother on the head.

When I came back in, I didn't see Stacey or Beth around so I figured they were probably doing their

homework. I was twirling on the kitchen bar stool when Stacey came into the room. She handed Mom a note. I leaned over the counter so I could read it, too. What a brain Stacey was! She calculated all the hours of the week she *didn't* watch TV (which were 90 hours out of 105 waking hours). I immediately chimed in. "I don't watch TV even more hours, Ma. I go to bed earlier than Stacey does." Stacey's brainstorm didn't even get a rise out of Mom. She was set on a TV-less week, no matter how brilliant her children were. She said, "I will not discuss this matter again, so resign yourselves right now."

Stacey resigned herself almost immediately. She just went back to

PROPERTY OF
CAMBRIDGE CITY SCHOOLS

St.Benedict Elem.Sch.Lib.

Chapter
1982 - 1983

doing her homework. Beth was already resigned. She didn't even come out of her room for the last pleading. I knew if the girls intended to get through the week without watching TV then I would, too. No sisters would last longer than me!

I didn't have any homework, so I wrote a letter to my cousin Frank. I asked him if I could come and visit because my mother was such a rat. I signed it, "Save me; your long lost cousin, Steve." It only took me two minutes to write the letter, so I wrote five other letters. They all said, "Save me"—even the one to my pen pal in Australia.

Mom was real cheery the whole night. Dad was a real cheery copycat. Stacey and Beth were cheery, too, but

I knew they were acting. No kid could
be cheery without a plugged-in TV.

Everyone read that night, except
me. I wrote another letter to Frank. It
said, "If you don't save me, I'll never
be your cousin again." I left everyone
reading and went to mail my letters.

The crickets' clicks were even
louder at night. I wished I could see
one of them. After I plopped my
letters in the mailbox, I started to
inch my way back home. I noticed a

star following me. I ducked behind a bush to escape that nosey star, but it was there waiting when I emerged.

Later that first night, I lay in bed and listened to the invisible crickets. I pulled my bed close to the window so I could check on that nosey star. And I wondered if the mice got away from the cats on the 5:30 show.

Day 2

ay Two without a TV
was almost a rerun of
Day One, except I did a few more
things. I didn't invite my friends. I
didn't feel like being kicked and
cramped in my room and running
out of snacks.

I oiled my baseball mitt. I made a lanyard for my whistle. I searched for the crickets and whistled for them, too, but I had no luck. I checked the mail to see if anyone wrote me back. And I acted cheery.

I did all that stuff and it was only four o'clock. So I knocked on Beth's door. She was chitchatting with Stacey but they let me in. I was glad they did because I didn't know what else to do. I had already asked Mom for dinner three times and she kept saying, "We eat at six."

"What are we going to do?" I said. "I'm going to go crazy way before Friday."

"Let's act out a game show," Stacey said. "I'll be the emcee and you two will be the contestants."

"I'm willing," Beth said.

I agreed, even though I knew I'd
lose. There wasn't anything better to
do anyway.

Stacey made up the rules—after
all, she was the gameshow expert. We
used Dad's alarm clock. Stacey set
the alarm ringing and when one of us
knew the answer, that person shut off
the alarm. Beth won the first two
rounds. I didn't know what continent
China was in or what the mountain
chain in Switzerland was. After the
third question, which was about
some river that flows through a rice
paddy in Indonesia, I quit. How long
could I take being a loser? I suggested
we chase each other around the beds.
They both nixed that idea, so I left
them to their chitchat.

I got into bed that second night, nearly two hours before my usual bedtime, and just stared at the ceiling. I considered sneaking down at 2:00 A.M. to watch the late-late show. Everyone would be fast asleep and they'd never know. And even if Mom caught me, what could she possibly give me as a punishment? I already had no TV to watch. After a little more thought though, I gave up the idea. *The Phantom of the Rue Morgue* was not the cheeriest thing to watch alone in a dark room at two o'clock in the morning.

I looked out the window. I couldn't

find that nosey star anywhere. I
hoped it hadn't followed someone
else home. No, that was silly. That
star was there somewhere, but I
couldn't see it.

I bet if I had a telescope I could see
it, I thought. I might even see the
crickets. A telescope would be like
my own private TV. I could tune in
anything I wanted. I could have way
more than thirteen channels, too. For
starters, I bet there were thirteen
thousand stars I could watch.

Anything going on at the moment
could be my soundtrack—clicking
crickets, rustling leaves, chirping
birds, screeching brakes. I guess I
decided right then I would have
something to do on Day Three. I
would build a telescope.

he next afternoon I raced home from school so I could start building. I didn't even have a snack or read *TV Guide*. I had to get right to work.

I knew telescopes were sort of cylindrical so I used two cardboard tubes—one large one from a paper towel roll and a smaller one from a toilet paper roll. I took apart my two magnifying glasses that I got from the machines at the supermarket and used them as lenses. I fit the smaller tube into the larger one. I was on my way.

But then how to keep the two lenses in place became a problem. The machines at the supermarket solved that for me, too. I chewed the gumballs I had saved from the machines and used the wads of gum to stick the lenses in place. I was going to have my own TV again, and in living color.

I painted "on" and "off" knobs on the tubes to remind me of a regular TV. My completed telescope was perfect, except for one thing. It only had a 1½-inch screen. I didn't care too much though. Only my eyeball had to fit in. And if the telescope worked right, the images would become ten times their real sizes!

By the time I finished my telescope, it was too dark to see a cricket and too light to see a star. Boy, nature sure goes about things slowly, I thought, as I waited for night to come. When night finally did come, it was so cloudy I couldn't see a thing through my telescope. The only thing left for me to do was go to bed. I even had blurred dreams that night.

Day 4

y Day Four, I was so anxious to use my telescope, I had almost forgotten what I was missing on the regular TV screen. Nature turned friendly and let the sun shine to light my world.

I grabbed my telescope and ran

23

outside to view my programs. With my naked eye, I noticed a bumble bee on our rose bush. It was time for an instant enlarged replay. I pulled the tubes back and forth in order to focus on the bee. Even I was surprised with what I saw.

My private screen formed an upside-down picture. A bee looks real funny napping wings down on a petal. A bird on a branch looks like it's flying upside down with a nest for

shoes. My telescope made every show a daytime comedy.

I was spying so hard through my telescope I even found my lost skate key hanging on one of the twigs of an azalea bush. I had been looking for that key ever since the last snow melted. My week was really starting to look up.

It took ages for Day Four to finally get dark. But I was ready when the first faraway star appeared in the sky. I had my telescope propped on the windowsill at a forty-five degree angle—just right for the prime-time shows. I peered through my telescope and discovered the sky shows looked right side up—a big difference from the upside-down daytime shows. Then I realized the night shows probably were upside down, too, but stars look the same right side up or upside down.

Just when I was focusing on a meteor, my cousin Frank called. He was ready to save me, but I was too busy to be saved. I told him to write me a letter and I'd answer it if I had time.

That night I dreamt that I discovered a new comet. I got all kinds of awards and medals and the president declared a school holiday to honor me. New York City threw a ticker-tape parade for me and it took the sanitation men three weeks to clean up the confetti.

Day 5

 n Day Five, I was ready to make my comet discovery. I knew I'd have to work fast, because at sundown I could plug in again. I only had five hours until my TV-less life was over. Unfortunately, I had to wait until it

got dark to survey the sky, so I used the daytime scenes to practice focusing. Stacey and Beth must have wondered why I wasn't bothering them for the past couple of days. They both followed me outside to check on what I was doing. As I darted around focusing on leaves and blades of grass, my antics got too much for them. "Let me see, too," Beth said. "Then me," Stacey said.

I could understand their feelings. How much homework could two sisters do without going stir crazy. I was the only brother they had with a lightweight portable TV screen that didn't need any plugs.

I taught them how to focus and told them to stop talking or we wouldn't hear any sounds. Stacey discovered an ant hill that looked like a cone with sprinkles all over it. Beth spied a caterpillar which we all took turns watching. We hoped we would see it turn into a butterfly.

When I took my fourth turn to watch the caterpillar, hoping I would see it make its change and fly away, a clap of thunder struck. The caterpillar hid under some leaves. "There goes the daytime star," I said.

"As a matter of fact, there go all the outdoor shows. It's going to rain any minute," Beth said.

She was right. The thunder got louder, lightning began to flash and the sky was dark enough to see a comet if there wasn't so much rain. I stuffed the telescope under my shirt. I didn't want to get the lenses wet. We all ran inside and peered at the buckets of rain that were washing away our live shows.

We were so busy watching the downpour through the kitchen window, that not one of us noticed that the refrigerator stopped humming. The storm had knocked out the power. It was not until my stomach growled and I went to get a glass of milk and a Twinkie that we

realized it. "There's no light in the refrigerator," I said.

Then Stacey flicked the wall switch and the overhead light didn't go on either. "The storm must have knocked out the power," Stacey said.

So we continued to watch the rain. I munched my Twinkie and Beth warned me to drink fast. She had heard no refrigeration could spoil food.

Then Mom came in to view the storm with us. "It's too bad the power had to blow just when you could plug back in again," she said, as she stared at the protrusion under my shirt.

"What lousy luck," I said. "No man-made shows and no nature shows either." I felt like screaming again.

"The rain has to stop eventually," Stacey said, "so let's be ready."

"What do you mean, 'ready'?" Beth asked.

"Well, Steve has a telescope. Let's make some more equipment to add to his." I always knew Stacey was brilliant. Of course, I didn't know what she had in mind, but I knew it would be a brainstorm.

Her ideas were even better than I had imagined. She scurried around searching for empty milk cartons and pocket mirrors. She was going to build a periscope so we could see around corners. Wow! I thought. With a periscope, I could surely find those hiding crickets. I came to her assistance with two candles, so she could find what she was looking for. After all, even a genius can't work in the dark.

Beth wanted to get into the act, too. "Do something to make the sounds from our shows better," I said. "It's awfully hard to hear crickets' clicks with a naked ear. And never once did I hear a caterpillar utter a sound."

"You're right, insect chatter must be fun to hear," Beth said. "But the only thing I can think of that makes sounds louder is a microphone and I sure can't build one of those. Besides, most microphones have to be plugged in and we have no power."

"Then build a megaphone," I said. "All you need for that is some oak tag. We'll just turn the wide part to the ground, catch the insect chatter and direct the sound to our ears."

Then I gave Beth another candle. I didn't want to play favorites. For all I knew, Beth might be a budding genius also.

As I was helping Beth fold the oak tag for the megaphone, Dad came home from work. "This kitchen looks like a real workshop," Dad said.

"Yeah," I said, as I pulled the telescope out from under my shirt. "This is invention number one."

"Looks good," he said, "except for
the gum." Dad was right. The
chewed gum was drying up and
losing its sticky power.

I got to work searching for a super
glue. What good was my telescope
with wobbly lenses or—worse yet—
no lenses at all. For my search, I used
a flashlight. All the candles were on
the kitchen table lighting up Stacey's
and Beth's creations.

I finally found some glue on the top shelf in the laundry room. Actually it was contact cement, but the tube said, "the ideal cement for thousands of around-the-house repair jobs," and that's sure what I wanted to do, so I used it.

We were so busy collecting, repairing and constructing, I never heard the refrigerator start to hum again. Our equipment was almost ready. I only had to wait two more minutes for the contact cement to dry and my lenses would be in place forever. It was getting dark enough for the sky shows, too.

But Mom heard the refrigerator hum. She flicked on the overhead light, and Edison's invention lit up our inventions. Stacey, Beth and I just stared at each other and no one said a word. The week without a TV was over and so was the power failure. We could switch on any program we wanted.

I looked at my watch. It was 6:30—time for the reruns. Then I looked outside and saw the sky was clearing. The reruns were O.K., but I could watch reruns any time. I was after a first run. Maybe I'd even discover a U.F.O. circling that comet this time.